VINCE FLYNN

EXTREME MEASURES

SIMON &
SCHUSTER

London · New York · Sydney · Toronto

A CBS COMPANY

First published in the USA by Atria Books, 2008
A division of Simon & Schuster, Inc.
First published in Great Britain by Simon & Schuster UK Ltd, 2009
A CBS COMPANY

1 3 5 7 9 10 8 6 4 2

Simon & Schuster UK Ltd
1st Floor
222 Gray's Inn Road
London WC1X 8HB

Simon & Schuster Australia
Sydney

www.simonsays.co.uk

A CIP catalogue record for this book is available
from the British Library

ISBN 978-1-84737-072-3

Designed by Rhea Braunstein

Printed in the UK by CPI Mackays, Chatham ME5 8TD